THE UNFAITHFUL WOMAN

ALEXANDER D. HOWARD

Copyright © 2022 Alexander D. Howard.

All rights reserved. No part of this book may be used or reproduced by any means, graphic, electronic, or mechanical, including photocopying, recording, taping or by any information storage retrieval system without the written permission of the author except in the case of brief quotations embodied in critical articles and reviews.

This is a work of fiction. All of the characters, names, incidents, organizations, and dialogue in this novel are either the products of the author's imagination or are used fictitiously.

LifeRich Publishing is a registered trademark of The Reader's Digest Association, Inc.

LifeRich Publishing books may be ordered through booksellers or by contacting:

LifeRich Publishing
1663 Liberty Drive
Bloomington, IN 47403
www.liferichpublishing.com
844-686-9607

Because of the dynamic nature of the Internet, any web addresses or links contained in this book may have changed since publication and may no longer be valid. The views expressed in this work are solely those of the author and do not necessarily reflect the views of the publisher, and the publisher hereby disclaims any responsibility for them.

Any people depicted in stock imagery provided by Getty Images are models, and such images are being used for illustrative purposes only.
Certain stock imagery © Getty Images.

ISBN: 978-1-4897-4070-0 (sc)
ISBN: 978-1-4897-4074-8 (e)

Print information available on the last page.

LifeRich Publishing rev. date: 03/02/2022

Prelude

Can you imagine falling in love with someone & creating so much together; all for it to later be destroyed by disloyalty, betrayal, & infidelity? To have all the promises, shared memories, sacrifices, commitments, & honesty thrown out the window by the very person you would picture to be the same as you were to them. To be made a fool out of & be stabbed in the back the deepest circumference from two people whom you believed would love you enough to protect your heart from such ache & pain. Never would've thought someone would be so evil as to try & demolish my life. To come for the one thing that I valued the most, my marriage. I loved you both, but you betrayed me in a way that could never be repaired.

This was an unpredictable act. It was done right underneath my nose. Like a sheep in wolf clothing, I was being done a bad hand. By my wife & my brother. How am I supposed to ever trust anyone again? How can I take another chance at love ever? I wanted forever with you, but you were willing to throw us aside just because of our normal marriage problems. I oftentimes wonder did I really slack on us that much, or did my looks & all just change for you? It is possible that you just married me for my wealth, are you in my family for the money or is it the name that you are after?

I do know the person you have shown me now, is not the person that I want in my life. I will heal with time, but we have come to a point of no return.

I

"The Special Day"

It was a warm spring morning of 2013 when I saw the most attractive, beautiful, & stunning person of my life. It was the way they had set my knee that I knew she was the right one for me. Her name was Isabella. She was the poor woman who lived on 531 Boulevard Street in the sophisticated city of New York. Her Mother and Father were not believers of god. They were Atheist, who believed in making their own way and had to just take things to achieve this lifetime. I, richest man of New York for which I was named, seen her in much of a need. Never ever did she seem or look like it to anyone.

She was cleaner that a diamond on an ornament for New Year's Eve! I adored her even though she was broke & wanted to marry her. She was the only poorest of the poor in New York and I was determined to keep her from all harm. We were very close friends in the third grade until her parents took her away to Vancouver for three long years that I hated. They couldn't stand me because I was a believer in god & hated the fact that she was starting to believe with me, so they took her away without even a proper goodbye Isabella left the city of New York. I used to wait & wait for a letter from her saying I will be back soon, but I never got that either. In fact, I don't even think she remembers me. One day soon Isabella Whitefield's will remember me again.

Down the street she goes every morning to work with her flashy dresses and perfect make-up. It makes me want to settle down forever & and let her spend my richest cash. She works at the lawyer's office just two blocks down & as is go to the coffee shop every morning to get my cappuccino I watch her walk that pavement. I always knew we would be a great, outstanding couple. Soon we will shine as one big happy family with kids and a perfect home.

II

"THE DEDICATED WORK PAYED OFF"

On a Saturday Morning at the city park, it happened to be there gazing at the beautiful buildings. And there she was, walking with her dog. I wanted to say hey there don't you remember me, but I was scared. Unfortunately my braveness stepped in and said "hey girl remember me!" She looked with an odd look and then her eyes opened wide and says "David Shubbard is that you from third grade"! At that time I really wanted to kiss her, but I had to show respect. Even though her eyes were like "you look SOOO good," I did what was appropriate instead. So I made my response "yea girl long time go see!" "Omg it's been ages, give me a hug you rascal!" Those words were exactly what I was waiting on, now if I could just some way take her out, but I'm not sure if she's really interested in me. I didn't want to be too pushy, it's worth a try. "We should go out to dinner sometime Isabella, I mean after all we need to make-up for all the lost time anyways." "Well sure that'll be nice!" with a delighted smile on her face. "How does eight o' clock Friday night sound?" "Perfect, no plans let's do it & see you then Dave!" "alright belle!" I stood with proudness as I watched her walk away with the wind blowing her hair, glowing her beautiful, red, hair color. Back home I went to play on my piano my great grandmother had left me before she died. She was 82 years old & believed in me especially for taking great care of valuable things. My brother Richard on the other hand disliked her and did drugs. No one could ever understand why my brother was so violent and disrespectful. Maybe it was because of the abuse our father used to put us through.

The Unfaithful Woman

He used to tell me to shut the door and close my eyes because my brother was in trouble. All I could hear in his room was screaming and belt slaps, he told me I was his favorite and that I never disrespected him so I barely got any beatings, but when I did they were bad. I just wonder in my bedroom sometimes looking at all our pictures wondering what went wrong. My father was a mean old man, he treated my mom wrong like she was a slave. He often comes to mind and then leaves like dust blowing off a car.

Maybe I should bring Isabella some flowers to work with a card. That would be romantic. "god I want us to fall in love!" Looking out of the tall building of New York thinking about her, I wonder if she's still that funny girl from high school? She used to tell the teacher (Mr. Tucker) that her dog ate up her homework, but I knew she was telling a lie because she always told me she didn't want to do her homework and that it was so hard. When first saw her I couldn't believe she was back. I thought she would never come back to New York. My mom always wanted me to be with her and said that she was perfect for me, her attitude was delightful to her. My mother died of cancer. No one knew about it until last minute, my whole life has had nothing but tragic events no one is here for me. Sometimes I feel so alone like a refrigerator with no food contained in it. I keep asking myself will I find love, or is it all just a big joke for me? It's like repeating the same thing everyday only without a family. Is it me or is it just the atmosphere, giving up feels like the answer in this problem. After all these women I've been through, I still haven't gotten any process. This time if I get broken, I'm completely done with love once and for all.

III

"The Night Out"

Hopefully tonight will be the magical night. Even though I don't feel like going out maybe this will change me up a little bit. "I made reservations at Baxter's; the food is great there!" "Oh great!" "What time?" Seven Thirty and right now its Seven so we better get going because it's a pretty good piece from here & we need to get there early to get a seat since they're going to be packed in there like little red ants. "So, you're taking me to one of those first class restaurants huh?" "Yea and it's very classy." Tonight, if I was going to try and see if she was the right one, I had to put her to the test, to see what's she's really like. I started up my Mercedes Benz c- class up as we walked toward my beautiful baby with that low-key purr. "Wow Dave ole boy what a nice ride you must be rich?" "Well, I can't brag, but I am settled." As we sped off into the interstate on I 60 passing the lit-up buildings, there was nothing but silence. Well as a matter of fact I felt good about her & I think she was fascinated. Suddenly, my favorite song came on the radio (Alicia Keys ft. Maxwell) Fire We Make. I turned the volume up a little. She seemed like she was saying "jackpot" In her head. "So how long have you been back to New York?" I spoke. "8 Months, I came back because the town I was in doesn't really have good paying jobs." "What town were you in again?" "Indiana!" "oh, yea that's right I remember when you left, I didn't even know you were gone until someone told me you had moved." "I know right, you've changed a lot since I last seen you." "you went from a skinny little boy to a sexy strong muscular man." "Why thank you Bella, I guess I have changed a little huh?" "A little try a lot!" "Ha ha great compliment."

I was nervous but didn't want to show it. This could be true love,

I thought but let's see what she's going to do next. We pulled up at the restaurant. "And here it is the best seafood restaurant in New York." "Oh, wow never been here before, is it safe?" "100 percent, but no need to worry Dave is here to protect you." "Thanks" "You're welcome anytime." As the valet drove my car away, we walked into the building. Inside was a water fountain and an elevator to go up to the Baxster's restaurant. "This is the Hotel part; the restaurant is on the 3rd floor." "This is where most of the actors and actresses come to stay when they're shooting a film." "Are you serious?!" "No joke, you'll run into many of them here." "Omg I would love to meet Halle berry!" "You're not the only one." Going up to the 3rd floor was a pretty good peace, then suddenly the elevator stopped and then the doors open to the most sophisticated restaurant in town. Inside the restaurant was people talking, laughing, and enjoying their meals. The waiter was getting ready to assist us, I had my order ready in my head. It was my favorite meatballs, but second thought I might as well get the buffet since we are together. "Hello there, my name is Suzanne what would you two like to order tonight?" I decided to answer first. "Yes I'll have the buffet tonight." "Alright and what would you like to order mam?" "Oh um... umm not sure do you know what they have here Dave?" "Tell you what it's on the house, I'm paying for her tonight & pay with it on my Chase credit card". "No Dave I can't let you do that!" "just let me do this Bella, tonight is your special night." If I was taking her out the least I could do is pay for the night out, and besides it's about respect anyway. The table by the window was always my seat. I loved sitting there just to look out at the city and relax. "Let's sit at the window it's my place to relax." "sure ok." To the buffet line I went after leaving my jacket on the seat. The most delicious foods you could ever want was at the buffet line. Boiled shrimp, Cocktail Sauce, Fish, Rice, Crab legs, & oh! The meatballs. Growing up in my childhood years, meatballs was me, my mother, and my brother's favorite thing to eat. My dad wasn't around as much as he should have been because he was in the army. Someway Somehow I think that was the reason why he was so abusive. I would never go into the army even if I lost every single dollar I have in my bank account and everywhere else. It messes with the mind and you can't get back straight. I just wish my father had of treated my brother better, maybe his life would have been different. He blew all his money away on drugs. The whole situation started when he was 21 years old and he had went to this club on East Avenue. He went into the club and he wanted to make some quick change because he was to lazy to go to college like me. So he sold some quick drugs and soon it became a reoccurring habit. Then one night Mother & I was sitting at our dinner table eating. Which we were both were worried about him & were wondering where he could be this late. The door soon opened and he came in and was stumbling with no balance, I ran up to him to catch him before he fell. And all I smelt was Crack Cocaine, I immediately broke down and said, "Oh My God!" "What have you done!" The only thing I could think about was that he could be addicted forever now. My mother was very scared and stunned and was walking up to see what was the problem. I quickly took my brother and said "Oh mother its nothing his clothes are just dirty and I need to take him to get some new wear and throw these away." "Can't have a bunch of dirt in the washing machine." She was blind but she could walk anywhere in the house because she was taught how to. Her name was Louise. She was left all alone at home while I was covering for my brother. I took him to a hospital and they immediately rushed him in for diagnostics. The test came back that he had cocaine in his system. The doctor said that he had enough in him to pull down a cow. And every since then, he's been stuck on it. No one has heard from him or seen him because he ran off to god knows where. If only I could see him now I would know how to help him but I was still a boy then.

After getting my food I went and sat down. I watched Isabella put the food she seem to wanted on her plate, and then she came to sit. "So what have you been doing all these years Dave, let's catch up." "Well I finished high school & then I went to college for law school." " Wow interesting I should've known you're so sophisticated and handsome, any woman would love to have you." "And any man would have a gold mine to have you." By that time I knew she was thinking of me because she blushed. "Why thanks but anyway, so where do you work." "I work at Global Wise Industries by the way I also spent a little time studying some business also." "That Is so much work you were determined." "Thanks now let's get to you there sweet cheeks if you don't mind." " sure go ahead why else are we here." "ight so what have you been doing all these years?" "well I went to college to as you must know, I am a Administrative Assistant." "Ah I should've known, the perfect assistant at a desk!" "It's not as easy as you think." "what do you do there?" "I take calls, take care of file papers, and show guests to the manager's office." "so where do you do this at"? "Capital One Bank." "I used to have an account with them a long time ago, but then I stopped using them, I should come visit sometimes, probably reopen my account also." "You should it'll be fun with me being your assistant and all." "yea it would." I think I should pay her a visit, maybe surprise her with a little flowers and some chocolate to help her at ease. Then take her to lunch for some coffee & chat about how the day at work is going so far. In my mind I had it planned out but I couldn't let her know because it was going to be a surprise. "So you enjoying your food?" "Dave this food is amazing, ad this restaurant is so full of sophisticated people." "This is the first time you've ever been to this restaurant?" "yea, but it's only because I don't get to this side of town much because I'm always busy with something." "That's all of us these days, I barely have any days off work here lately." "I know right and I'm ready when you are." "ok just let me go to the bathroom and then we'll hit the road". We both were done eating now so I went to the bathroom to freshen up before we left. She seemed just right, and for far as I can tell perfect for me.

IV

"The kiss and Surprise"

We checked out of the restaurant & waited for the valet to pull the car up front. Tonight was the best night I have ever had in years. To be honest, I think I'm in love. The car was pulled up in front of us, & I opened the door for her to get in. "Get on in my sweet dear." "Thanks Dave." The valet gave me my keys to my car and I told him thank you have a nice night. I got into my white beauty and drove off, I call her white beauty because she's pearly white and shines from all angles when clean. "I enjoyed our eat out tonight." "Me to I enjoyed talking to you, after all these years we should do this again." "yea that'll be great I'll let you know when I have another free off day so we can get together again." "ok sure." We pulled up at her apartment. I got out of my car and went to the other side to open the door for her. "See you later." She said and kissed me on my cheek. "And we really should do this again Dave." Stunned by the kiss she just gave me on the cheek I answered. "Ok have a great morning, I mean night!" She waved at me as she went in her house. I got into my car and couldn't even move from that sweet peachy kiss. I could feel the heat running through my body like fire and ice combined and then strikes like a lightning bolt coming at 100 miles per hour. It made me want to go in her house and make her spend a long night with me at my house with the lights off. We could cuddle and watch movies and I could be her teddy bear. She was definitely getting a present from me tomorrow if that was the only present she got from anyone.

 I just couldn't stop thinking about that kiss last night. Some chocolate and flowers would do nice for her, so down to the florist shop I go. I went to Kendal's gift shop on the corner of 1111. "hey my name is David and

I'm looking for some lily flowers and chocolate." If I was going to buy some flowers, they were going to be the best smelling and the prettiest. "Sure right this way sur." "here are our Lily flowers right here!" "How much are they?" "Twelve dollars each, they're on sale for 15% off." "Great I'll take them." Anxious to take them to her, I immediately took them right after I left the store. The traffic was busy & I needed to get there before she left for break so I pulled over and walked. Finally getting to the bank I walked in I asked the assistant for Isabella Haynes. As soon as I did there she was coming around the corner. "hey Dave what are you doing here?" "Bella I'm here to bring you this."

"Oh Dave what's this for?" "I think you deserve this Bella." "No Dave, you don't have to do this for me." "take it because you were on my mind this morning." "Awe thanks Dave, you know you mean a lot to me." "You're welcome anytime." "ok." "So I know it's almost time for you to go to lunch break and all and I was kind of wondering.." I was scared to ask her, what if she said no and make me feel bad. Come on David it doesn't hurt to try. "yes Dave?" "Well you see I was wondering for your lunch break if we could go to the park & sit at the lake and probably have a picnic lunch." She looked as if she were saying "oh my god I can't believed he just asked me this." "Sure Dave and I'll guess I could leave early it's only 5 minutes so why not, just let me go get my coat." "ok I'll be waiting for you right here." I was happy she said yes. She's starting to make me feel different, like a new man. I can't explain it but it feels like I want to run freely. Sitting down waiting on her to come back down so we could leave for lunch, I was looking at all the rewarded bankers who had worked there for so many years. I was keeping myself occupied. All the people who came in the bank were rich just like me. They talked professional like me, walked kind of like me, smelled with the most expensive perfume like me, and rode in sexy top class vehicles like me. "I'm back are you ready to go now?" "Why yes my darling." I answered with romance and complete class. "So where do you want to go?" "Let's go to the Cunningham's park, but first we'll stop by the store and get a sheet and some picnic goods." "Sounds like a great idea I'm down for whatever." We were heading to the street which was filled with traffic & we had to wait for the sign to say go. I was going to help her across the street. "Take my hand and we'll just walk across together." "Um ok Dave you're so nice." "Thanks I get that a lot." "I know you do with that sweet face & that pretty smile." "And I know you get plenty of flowers with that sexy personality & the way you carry yourself." Whether she knew it or not I was flirting with her. I wanted to love her, but I knew for a fact we needed to get to know each other more before I tried to make that step. "Thanks Dave you're the best." "You're welcome anytime." We had arrived at the grocery store. Into the double doors we went. The store was full of people buying food because It was check day, and here in the city check day is more busy than just a medium town like Georgia for example. Out here in New York at the first and third of the month, the stores are full like a riot over the whole city. "This store here has the best food for picnics like bologna, sandwich meat, & condiments to make the food taste better, & plus it's quick to get in and out because there are self-checkouts here." "Great because I hate being in a crowded store and most of the cashiers are on break knowing they have a pile of customers, that just burns me!" "You're not the only one it burns, one day I had to put my contents back and leave."

"I don't blame you." "So a peanut butter and jelly sandwich would be good to have on a picnic, especially a quick one." "Yea and a Kool-Aid patch, I haven't had one in years, let's get these and put it in the basket Dave." "AL righty and we can take these Newton Figs also." "Ok you ready because I am?" "Let's get out of here." Walking past all the other shopper in the store was a bit of time consuming because she had an hour of lunch to spend freely & we had already spent 15 minutes of it walking and shopping for the things we needed. I'm the type of man to do things quickly, but efficiently also so that it is done fast and perfectly. I would have asked her to the bar, but I thought that wouldn't be appropriate considering that it was only the second date. Maybe the third date I could take her there. We were at the cash register line now and there were only two people getting checked now so that was a great fit in.

"I told you we'd be out in no time." "Ha yes & I'm glad you brought me here & told me about this place now I'll come here from now on." "Yes no one should have to spend their day in a grocery store, it's a waste of time."

V

"Date Number Two"

It was only five minutes of waiting in line. We were out of the store in no time & that left us with forty five minutes of picnic time. I haven't been on a date this many times with the same woman in years. The last time I've been on a date was five years ago. We had to break up because she decided that she liked women & that she wanted to be honest with me so that was it. I had given up on love, but when I saw that she'd came back, I knew I had a shot.

Walking up to the gate of the park, we went into the peaceful place where the sun was beautifully glaring on the pond. "This is the park here." I said to her while searching for a spot. "Wow it's, so beautiful here I've never been here, it's a shame I been missing out on things like this." "I can understand you work and all, you'd be surprised of the busy work you have to do." "I barely get any sleep les known if I had kids." "Tell me about it." "So what's to eat for the picnic?" "Apples, Grapes, peanut butter & jelly sandwich, & some bread." "Yum Yum! I get to go back to work and tell my co-workers my lunch was outside while theirs were inside!" "Ha ha so what's it like at your job?" "A lot of work, sometimes I have to stay all the way until 3:00 o' clock at night." "exactly, and then end up taking a nap there because you fall asleep." "yes." I heard something coming really fast & I turned around and looked. As soon as I did a dog on a leash came straight through me and the chain caught my throat. "Dave! Are you ok?" Isabella said while running towards me. Grabbing the chain on the dog pulling it away from my throat because it was choking me, finally she caught the dog and unwrapped the chain from my neck. "Dave I'm so sorry, are you hurt!?" "Nah I'm fine It's just my throat from the chain."

I said softly. "Who does this dog belong to, because I'm sure they would come looking for it now, since it's not in their sight." "You're right." I was listening to her, but all I could think about was the time. We only had 15 minutes left which left us with 10 minutes because it took 5 minutes to get her back to work. Just as I was looking at the watch, the owner of the well groomed dog came up. "I am so very sorry for my dog guys. I don't know what got into her she just looked up and started barking and running away." "It's ok ma'am it wasn't any trouble, no big deal." "Thanks, now come here Patricia, why did you run away from me? Again guys I'm really sorry for the troubles have a nice evening." "Thanks you to!" we both said as she walked away with the dog with her. "Considering we only have 14 minutes left now, we do have enough time to sit down and eat a quick peanut butter and jelly sandwich if nothing else." "Yes let's do that & chat quickly since time is blowing over so fast." Sitting down on the picnic blanket, I started making the sandwiches for the both of us. In my mind I was thinking when the right time to pop the question was, but I decided to wait a few minutes. "so Dave have you been working hard here lately?" "well yea making new things happen trying to make the company more known that's a job." "Yea I can feel you, especially during the holidays." "Yea so I want you to tell me what the kiss meant last night." "What?" "I want you to tell me what the kiss last night meant when I brought you home from the restaurant?" "Oh, Yea, that, Um I was just being friendly." "Friendly huh?" I said while having a charming look on my face. "Yea, so it's about time for us to start heading back to the bank before I'm late & you know how that is."

"Well alright ladies first." "Ha Dave, you're the funniest person I've ever met." "I know." I knew that kiss was more than just being friendly, but I played it cool like I went along with it. Every time she looked at me, she wanted me more. I'm up to exactly what she's playing which is hard to get, but I wasn't ready to bring the magic touch yet. "So you want to do this again Bella?" "Oh, Yea, sure." "I just want to say that I really enjoyed today Bella, it's been so interesting being with you learning things and all." "Thanks I've been enjoying you also Dave. You're so charming and funny, I can't even remember the last time I've been on a date this many times with a man." "The last time I went on a date was when I graduated high school, now you know that's a shame." "Don't be embarrassed, I have no room whatsoever because the last time I went was before I left here. And I was what, 13 then possibly?" "Yea because you had some girl issues then, I remember when your dad came to get you out of school that day because of that." "Wow you remember that, I was so devastated I didn't know what was going on with me!" "yea and you were screaming and running through the halls." "ha." As she was laughing, we turned to each other and her Ocean Blue eyes connected with mine & we then got closer & closer to each other. I touched the side of her face and trembling I leaned over to kiss her. "Dave I'm sorry I just can't, Um! Can we talk later? I'll call you." She ran into the bank and got on the elevator. Watching the door close, I turned around. "You can run but you can't hide Isabella." I walked away from the bank windows stirring up a plan to comeback with.

VI

A Plan in the Making

I definitely had a plan; I just hadn't put all of the pieces together yet. Somehow, Someway, I had to get her to admit that she was in love with me. Her game was good, but mine was better. Gazing out the window at the city, I couldn't help but to think about her. To be honest I feel nervous about the whole thing. The next date I was thinking about, could be a nice, relaxing, evening out playing tennis. The eating out is kind of getting over baring. She probably was getting that way also.

If we were really going to be together, there was only one secret that I had to tell her about. It was about my past. Living a life on the run is not good at all, in fact it's not a life and it makes no sense. You barely get any sleep and you have to keep a low key on every move you make & watch out for the people who may go and report it. And well, let's just hope you have their money because if you don't then you will more than likely be punished in a crucial way. The date is the deadline and if you don't have all of the (dough) as they call it, then you are going to pay the piper & pay it hard. The only way you can get away from something like that is if you escape without a word from and to anyone & move miles away. You have to dodge the intensity of being in contact with anyone.

I distinctly remember to this day I was running away from the feds, because of this. It was a life threatening and unloving situation. No one to this day knew how I made it through college with nearly not a dime too spare. The secret was that I was a drug dealer & a convict.

VII

The Big Q

The question I needed the answer to was an important question, and that question was how was I going to tell her about this? I mean if I don't tell her then she will find out eventually anyway. This is a have to tell thing or get nailed. The last time I kept a secret from someone I loved I got dumped and I can't, I repeat can't let this happen again because of my ego. My mother always said to me "your daddy ruined you with pride." She is so correct I experience it every time I get into a problem. I must be honest at the start before we get serious because I can feel the sexual tension between us. I want an honest & loving woman, and I wasn't to be and honest and loving man. I should be her knight and shining armor, but she won't let me if I'm keeping secrets from her. Somehow, Someway, She must know.

Getting dressed for work I go putting my suit, shoes, & jewelry on. I had to be in by 9:30 and it was nine o' clock which meant, that I had fifteen minutes to get to work because I always come an extra five minutes early to clock in & then go to my room. So I quickly got my books together & went into the bathroom to the mirror to check to see if I was on point with every detail. It was great. In my car I go and get on the freeway to work in a good mood, hoping today will succeed for me in all the right places.

VIII

What's Done in the dark comes to the light

Sitting at my desk at work thinking about how I was going to tell her about my darkest secret, she comes into my office and slaps me. "How could you not tell me about your dope selling, as if I wouldn't find out, how stupid do you think I actually am David?!" Stunned that she called me David, I answered back with a crack inside my voice. "I—I was going to tell you, but I didn't know how." "Oh, you liar, I can't believe I thought u were a honest person, you are sick!" "Listen I really meant to tell you in the best of intentions without you being hurt!" "Save it David I'm done…. I don't ever want to see you again you got that!" She walked out violently; I did not get to defend myself at all. All my Coworkers in the office now looking at me with their mouths wide open. Embarrassed, I leave the office and head home, calling her phone trying to talk to her, but every time I call, it goes to voicemail. She really caused a scene and embarrassed my reputation at work, but who cares I just want the woman I love to not be mad at me, that's right I said it, I love her! I regret that I even kept my truths from her in the first place… My Brother has been out to get me since Our Father died, and I don't understand why he Is angry at me. I know he blames me for Our father abusing him… but the truth is, I believe my father would've killed us all had I tried to help my brother. My Father was very weird, I thought as a child. As he got older, he started doing things that were unexplainable, like one day he killed a pet rooster and put it in a Ziploc bag, then put it in his refrigerator. Far as I know it stayed in there for a month or so, because the refrigerator for him was also in his shed, because we had a garden in the backyard so he'd decided he would build a shed and put useful things on the inside to help with the garden, but after

I last seen the rooster in the shed, I went back out at the beginning of the month to get some squash for mom to cook, and the rooster was gone. I assumed that dad ate it, along with the cat he killed also and stuck in the freezer. Now we all know no one really talks of eating a cat, so I really was sketchy about my father. My Brother and I were very distant from him because he drank a lot and which that made him very mean at times. He was incredibly quiet, never really had any friends that I know of. Mr. John & Mrs. Lean were nice, but they were our neighbors. They especially made sure they visited on the holidays, because in my neighborhood everybody brought each other a dish or two for the holidays and wished each other happy holidays. My Mother pretended like we were a big happy family like they were for a while, but as the years went by it was clear she was tired and burned out of playing Ms. Perfect & trying to satisfy my father, though most of the time it would always backfire on her. It was as If he did not want to get along with my mother. He would often leave us home and stay gone for a week or two, with no explanation as to why. Bottom Line is no one is perfect.... there is no such thing as "perfect." Devastated about today I take my clothes off, turn on the shower, & get my bathing accessories together. I checked my phone to see if she had possibly called, which was a dumb move, because she had not. I wonder if I can come to work tomorrow or am, I permanently fired. The truth is I was a little wild in the streets also, like my brother. It is sad, I used to sell drugs, & my brother is on drugs. It was either come off the streets for good, or I will end up dead literally…or in jail. One day I went to this specific neighborhood for distributor (the guy who provided us with the drugs & gave us half of the money), to sell a bag to someone. I was supposed to meet the guy in the ally of an old hospital, but it turned out vastly different. I made the complete wrong decision, one so, that today I could be in jail for an exceptionally long time, or I could be six feet under. The mishap was that I had given the drugs to an undercover cop.

IX

"Saved by the Bell"

The undercover cop had to be tipped off about me from someone, because this was a place where usually there were not any cops, this was at a very late time even the crickets couldn't have been stirring, & the guy that I knew that had told me that the person needed some, was the same guy who showed me the ropes to making the money. I guess he felt that I was taking his shine in the neighborhood, so he gave me up to the feds. Just how do you give someone to the feds, but you are the orchestrator of all the illegal trafficking? We could have at least talked it out of he felt so intimidated by my sales or commission. Sitting in the interrogation room I felt betrayed by a person that I thought was my friend. The whole time they were against me and conspiring towards me. I never figured someone could become jealous of one if they have gotten to know them so well. "So, how long have you been trafficking exactly?" The investigator said as he was walking over to sit in front of me. "I am going to need for you to be completely honest & straightforward with me, at this point it would be for the best." "I have been ever since I've graduated from high school." I knew that the least I could do was be honest. I was at rock-bottom and I am quite sure that my life would never be the same after today. It seems that all at once I'd lost everything and all that was in my path that were at least going right or at least well, had fallen apart at my own hands. I had nothing to lose now I had self-sabotaged my own life. "What was it that made you get into this game fresh out of high school?" Oh shit, I just knew that he would ask me that question. This was the story that I really was not prepared to face, the one that It has taken me years to come to a term with. "My father was very abusive to me along with a drinking

The Unfaithful Woman

problem & he had thrown me out of the house after trying to help my mother from being abused by him." In my mind I am thinking now is this a therapy session because I had never really told anyone this. "So, you had no other choice but to do something In order to not live on the streets at the time am I right?" "Yes, it was to either eat or to be eaten, I basically was homeless if I hadn't of done something, I probably wouldn't be who I am today." I somehow always knew that one day if I did not stop before it was too late; that I would be caught up in some messy exchange. The sad part is that I never thought that it would happen when it had. Really, I was a lost little boy still when I left home unsure, fragile, broken little boy. I had my mother on my mind each day that I did not speak to her. Wondering was she really ok, should I have went back, wishing that she would just leave, praying for her to obtain the strength to know that she deserved better. I miss Isabella, I really felt that we had a connection with each other. I want to call her up, but I am afraid of rejection. I don think she would ever want to speak with me again at this point after everything that happened. She was indeed the one for me her eyes, the way she walked, talked, her persona she was giving me everything. A strong, beautiful, confident, intelligent woman. "Alright Dave, here is the deal I will let you go." "Do you mean that I am not going to prison?" "Dave, would you like for me to put you into prison? Or would you like to be free with a second chance of an abundant life, I will let you choose." "Thank you so much officer you don't" "hush dave", he said as he started to explain to me that talking too much could be a giveaway and add to a deeper investigation of something that I could be blessed out of. "There was no evidence of you actually committing the crime, so I am going to have to let you go as I did not see anything for myself. You can thank me later, but just get your ass out of here and I do not expect to see you back here. You kids could be so much more and I see it in you Dave, do not let this opportunity to do better in life slip from your hands and you end back here with your reputation and life damaged for eternity. I will be watching you and I also expect to see you do better. Between you and I, If you need anything from me I am more than happy to help you out. Just get yourself together, the streets are not healthy for you nor are they built for you Dave. I will see you around, he winked at me as he opened the door to the interrogation room and proceeded to direct me out of the police station. I just walked towards exiting the station, I was thankful but at the same time, in my mind I was saying what in the hell just happened? Did he really just let me get off for this after I thought that I would face serious charges for this? God really shined on me and my situation today, he worked through that officer to be generous enough to this situation just for me to have a second chance at life and opportunity. I had no doubt that he was giving me a sign, and now I knew that this route was not the route that is destined for me.

"The Call"

It's evening. The crickets are chirping, I can hear the water flow from the river near my apartment as I sit out on the balcony trying to clear my head. I am not sure what made me think that the "quick way out" was the easy way out. If I ever was to have anything honest and prospering out of life, I knew that I needed to work for it and by doing this I simply were only wasting time now that I look back, there so much more that I could've been doing to reach closer, but this is where I am now and I can't afford to waste another second. I picked up my pc and began to do research on investment banker interns. I did take accounting and business classes in high school, but I didn't finish the courses into college, as I had started subsequent to graduating high school. There is a part of my life that I have not released to anyone. I lived with my grandmother in Constance, a town an hour and a half away from my parents after I left their home. She had taken me in where it was safe and I were more comfortable, but my main concern was my mother though at the same time only she could make the decision to leave. I mourned her each day, just wanting her to come with me where she would not be mistreated. I missed her just reading me bedtime stories at night and loving on me before I went to sleep. There were days where we would just go to the park or to the movies, her, I, & my brother and we would just do whatever. We would laugh and talk for hours, even my dad before he became the alcoholic he had turned into. I missed our family, it crumbled before my eyes. My grandmother helped me get into college. I loved learning about being an entrepreneur and businessman. It was my lasts 2 years of college that I had to withdraw, I had become unable to pay so I had no other choice but to drop or to owe money. My grandmother's credit was not good enough to apply and become eligible to help me. That is kind of how I got set on the wrong path from there and forward. Not having the support of my father because he was an addict, really had been heartbreaking for me and looking back now there still is a void in my life. Without him, I feel less of a man, less of a "breadwinner" as they call it. He was not there to teach me how to finesse a woman, how a woman should be treated, how to nurture a woman. Obviously, you would think by the things that I have said he was as an "addict" that he would not be a prime example of showing me those things, but my "sober" dad, the man I knew before he became an alcoholic, the one before he became abusive to my mother, brother, and myself was quite the opposite. He was caring, loving, inspirational and a man of integrity. That was the man that I looked up to, he was the man that I admired and wanted to be. All of the things about him the way he carried himself, the way he spoke, dressed, all of it screamed that he was the man that people respected. The tables turned, and I just never understood what made him change to the man that I at least last knew that he was.

Beep-beep, my phone rings. I snapped out of the flashbacks and I get up from the balcony and I procced to go upstairs and check my phone. Exhausted and overwhelmed from today, I really do not want to have a conversation with anyone, none of the less speak to someone with any bad news or that will make me anymore unhappy and disappointed that I am with myself at this moment. I open the bedroom door, walk towards my dresser. My phone is flashing with my favorite ringtone. I pick it up, the screen displays an unknown number on my phone, answer it the spirit tells me. I rarely ever have gotten an unknown call. I do not remember when the last time had been since I have received a call that is, as some folks call it "a star 69 call." "Hello" I answer softly, in a puzzled persona as to being cooperative to finding out who this person could be. "Hi" the other party says. "May I ask who this is, you have called me unknown, the least you could do is state a name along with your hi." "David, it's me." "Name please if you will I know a lot of people, so me could mean a quite few people." "Dave……it's Isabella."

XI

Baxster's

I am floored. Did I just receive a call from the woman that I believed that I would never hear from again? Am I dreaming? I was sure that she was finished with me for good after she had found out about my dirty past. I just knew she had judged me for that one incident just like all the others and disregard me. "Dave, are you there?" I snapped out of it; I had gone to the wonder land in such whammy. "yes, I am here, I did not think that I would be hearing from you again." "Dave, could we meet and talk, I do want to say over the phone that I apologize for the way I carried out and for no hearing you out before making a preconceived notion, how does Baxster's tomorrow at eight o'clock sound??" "Sure, that sounds great." I said with a great deal of disbelief.

"I look forward to seeing you there Dave." "Me too Is." That was all that I could say, the way that she was upset with me, I never in a million years imagined that she would ever have spoken with me again. I only could sit on my bed and just think, wow my prayer is answered. The angels must have all the stars in line for me. I like her a lot hell, I may even love the bitch, but one thing is for sure I cannot let this chance slip. This time, it might be the end for good. She makes me smile uncontrollably when I think of her. She brings me into the light, she's my strength to strive more, my guide, my everything. She will be all mine soon, there will not be a thing to keep us from being what is destined for us. That woman is my eye, and I will most definitely be her thief in her knight. I will gain her trust and show her that I am just what she needs and all the security she will ever need to desire for.

Tomorrow, I must start to figure out what I will be wearing, how I exactly will look, all of it. I want to walk in, and I want her to show her expressions right on her face. It is my mission to be unforgettable to her.

I have a busy day early tomorrow, but I have to fit a few things in to make sure that I am at my best and bring my best for 8pm. This chocolate shall be visible and fully desirable for her to indulge in. One so rich that she will shake at her thighs and legs.

XII

"Rekindling"

The sun has risen, my alarm goes off. I hit snooze and stretch in my king size bed as I open my eyes to the beautiful NY city daylight. Today is one of those days where there are arons to be ran, including preparing for tonight. I hop out of bed and head towards the shower, turn on my jbl speakers and set my water to a pleasant temp.

 I need to apologize to Is for not telling her upfront what my past were. I honestly was embarrassed to tell her about my past. She seemed so well respected and well established with her name that I really felt intimidated to tell her anything about my past struggles. I only was concerned about impressing her, but I guess sooner or later that can all run dry if you are not being honest about everything. As I am in the shower bathing my body down, I imagine us in the shower together, me twirling my fingers up her thighs and clit. Giving her all that she desires from me, making sure that she is not dissatisfied but all the opposite from a daddy like me. I want to fondle her until she lets me know that I own her and not just her body, her mind, soul, and spirit to.

 The way that I would eat her and the things that I would perform on her would take her breath completely away. She would never want to leave me. I am not sure if she is a virgin or if she has experienced sexual healing before, but whether she has or not, she has not had an experience until she gets a taste of her daddy. Tonight, will be the night that she will become fully aware of how I can please her. Tease her as well. I hop out of the shower, the slow, sexual music playing in the background I start to fix my hair in the mirror, which I need to get trimmed up for tonight.

 I must go to the office and get my things if I am fired, which I am not sure and I guess I will find out once I drop by today since I have not gotten a call from my boss or a text. I will be a little embarrassed to walk in, I don't know what my co-workers will do once they see me probably tease or possibly make a huge scene and have all of the attention brought to me. One thing that is more important at this point is that I get to see my girl. So, fuck what they say or think, but I have a surprise for their ass once they find out I snatched my lady back into my arms. I mousse my hair down and I head to my closet to find something to wear to the office.

I think I will just wear my blue slack and my dress shirt; I do still want to "dress the part" as they call it. I grab my LV shoes from my top shoe shelf, and I sit on my bedroom chair beside my dresser stand. "Oh, I almost forgot!" I get up in a hurry and sprinkle on a Tab of my Michael khors for my smell and rush back to put my last shoe on and head out. Down the elevator I go to my apartment and head outside to the parking lot to my Mercedes c-class Benz. Yes, I love my Benz I remember when I first saw it on tv, and I had to have it. It was in a champagne color with a sunroof and all the above. It struck my eye and had just come out and then next day I went to the dealership and took it for a test drive, then could not resist leaving without it; so, I bought it right then and there.

I pushed the button to start and it welcomed me as I buckled up and headed out of the ally. The office was approximately a twenty-minute drive from my apartment. I lived downtown on the west side of New York while the office was located on the east side. The traffic was easygoing this morning. It is still morning rush hour today as people head to work, school, and wherever their destination is.

I always play uplifting music in the mornings, especially while I am driving on the interstate. It seems the time and drive go by faster than any other kind of tune. Welp, there is someone who has been stopped by an officer on the interstate. That is the usual every other day, better than an accident which holds traffic up and makes you later to reach your destination. If they are hurt, you might as well call and say you will be at least 30-45 minutes behind the schedule.

Being only 5 minutes away from my usual exit to the office; I am getting a little weary about walking in. A little ashamed as well. Either way I must go in, so I need to just be bold and nonchalant with my integrity in full force. Pay the peasants no mind as they say, for they are not aware of the path you have walked.

I take the exit to the office. I can see it as the big skyscraper that it is from the street over. I approach the red light to turn onto the street, turn into the parking ally, and proceed to park in my usual space. The space is still empty as far as I can see because I parked here every day, so I wonder what awaits me as I walk in. I've entered the double doors and I tap the level up elevator selection to go to the top floor. The door opens, I enter the elevator and press floor 3. As the door proceeds to close, a woman runs around and retracks the door to enter inside. "Hooo, I am glad I caught that last minute, I am running behind!" she said as she turned around. It happened to be carol, one of my co-workers on the top floor.

"Dave! It's you! What happened with you the other day?!" she asked in curiosity and prostration. "If you don't mind carol, I would really like to not even discuss it at this moment." "ok, well it is great to see you back, I wasn't sure if you had left for good or what!" "Well, it is great to see you as well carol, looking beautiful and brilliant as always." I responded to her while thinking in my head at the same time I think you may not be seeing me here again, but I chose not to say that aloud because I really was not sure nor was, I really willing to discuss that.

"We have a frantic day ahead of us Dave, I will see you at lunch I guess." She says as the doors open to the 3rd floor of the office. Hold and behold, the doors open to a "typical" busy day at the office. People on the phone, at the fax machine, on the computer, in the lounge room having meetings. My eye lies directly towards my boss, Richard's office. My feet began to pace towards his office to speak with him, as I see him there as usual sipping his coffee and reviewing his portfolio. My hand reaches the handle to the glass door. He raises up and sees me "Dave" he says as always "Rich" I responded back, "So I am here to speak with you about the other day." "ok, have a seat." He says as he relaxes his portfolio and draws his complete attention towards me. "I would like to first sincerely apologize for what went down and that was something that I had no idea would occur. I have been through some things in my past, but I never intended for them to be spilled into this office." He sits in his chair and stairs at me from what looks like blank for a few seconds and says "Dave, are you really serious right now? You really are embarrassed by that little simple incident, aren't you??" I couldn't help but to look at him with a though in my head like, what in the hell are you talking about? Of course, that's embarrassing, but instead I just said "yea, it really was for me do you not think that it should be for me rich??" "what I'm saying Dave, is everyone in this office has a story including myself, that we may not speak about, advertise, or put out on front street, but its always there. Not one person in this office can judge anyone no more than the other so, therefore everyone here in this office live in the present moment and work as a team with the success and knowledge that we have and do what we do." "Three days have come by and I haven't heard from you." I said to Richard waiting on my verdict of the status of my current employment. "What about hearing from me dave? There's nothing for me to say." "Ok, am I fired or am I not because I imagined that I would pretty much be, I just came here to pick up my last paycheck and to clarify." It seemed as if we were playing a game of checkers with each other, rather than just cutting to the chase so someone had to at some time correct? "Dave no you're not fired what would make you think such a thing you are an asset to us it would take a lot for me to lose you." "If we did lose you it would be a demise of this company." Hearing Richard assure me that I have not lost my job gave me a sense of relief and also, a sense of a little less embarrassment secretly. I make great income here and most of my accomplishments and promotions in my career came from this company. "rich, you really are a lifesaver I don't know what I would do without you. I owe you one, we should catch up sometimes maybe some drinks or cocktails." "sure dave, I look forward to that now get to work today is one of those hectic days as you can see it's good to have you Back." I get up from the desk and proceed to exit Richards office into mine. As soon as I get to my desk and get seated into my desk chair Sarah comes in and hands me some documents. "hi David, here are some documents for you to look at. Today has been crazy as hell so far and it has just gotten started, I guess we should say an extra prayer and moment of silence huh?" she says as she stares at me with a smirk of laughter and distress both at the same time on her face. "yea, you may be right about that Sarah." I responded back with a nod and a smile. She always seemed quite the helper of mine throughout my years of being executive here. She has been here for at least 6 years and has been promoted twice already based on my recommendations. She reminds me of iz with the way that she takes control of her work and her persona. She has great confidence in herself. It is almost as if she knows exactly what will get the attention when she takes over. Watching her walk back to her desk as I start to review the documents of the day with the cup of coffee sitting at my desk, I turn to my computer and start entering data for our daily accounts receivable. I only have 3 hours here and then I must leave to prepare for tonight. I have not even picked out what I will wear or anything. I have a 3pm hair dress appointment, a fitness class that I may just cancel at 6, and then the meeting with iz. Page after page I review and document after document I enter.

Once I finished, I only had 30 minutes left at work. Things seemed to have slowed down since this morning, as we do only have 2 more hours left before the day officially ends. "guys I'm shutting it down here today! I have some other things to attend to!" I say to everyone as I turn the lights off to my office and walk out of the door. "Goodbye dave!" everyone says as I walk out of the office and towards the elevator. I thought it was weird that no one asked me anything about what had happened. Maybe Richard set up a meeting and told everyone not to even mention it. Or maybe they all just decided not to even ask to make me comfortable, but whatever happened it sure did make me more comfortable because I really do not want to speak of it. Especially currently, one day I will have to just be more open about my life and just let go of my shame. Some things I just place in the back of my mind and behind me without speaking of it. I could probably be more successful if I did tell my story. The thought of having dinner on the deck by the ocean is a great relaxation, more in the summertime because everything is just more enjoyable and beautiful. You get to hear and see the dolphins and the ocean. The selection of food is just a delightful menu to choose from. I am a big seafood individual; so, I love to indulge in a little crab legs, shrimps (boiled or however), fish, and all of those good things. The elevator opens to the first floor, the lobby is cleared and there is complete silence. There is not much sun left as the skyscraper is blocking it, but it is very much warm and sunny.

It is 30 minutes before we meet, and I am dressed and ready to hit the road. There I stood 6'2, fine as hell, with the scent of a rugged but fierce male with dark black hair straight and shined laid backwards with white teeth and clear skin. Fine and sexy enough to hydrate all of the deserted animals and creatures in the mid-summer heat wave during

100+ temperatures with a cool and fresh breath of an Niagara Falls forest to make any woman fall to her knees in pleasure and desire with all but holy intentions, I was ready. I use a little tap of tress Emme hold spray, give myself a wink in the mirror, smile once ore to make sure there was not any food in between my teeth, brushed around the fresh cut areas of my mustache taking pleasure of my narcissism with my hand and then out of the door I went. I could just feel and smell my scent as I walked through the air.

Down the alley I went. I tap the keyless access to my benz, which I had freshly cleaned earlier and hop inside, opened the sunroof, and there I headed out to the restaurant. I tune my stereo system to Chris brown's "take you down." I am ready, more than ready for what tonight holds and not just for me, but mostly for her. She will be aware for sure of how much she needed for me to be in her life. The restaurant is only 9 miles from my apartment, which only takes approximately 10 minutes with normal traffic speeds.

The traffic did seem relatively fair and light this afternoon. After all, it was a Tuesday so all of the work and schooling traffic had surpassed which is mostly the only traffic that runs rapidly during the weekdays. The skyscrapers were lit and bright through the city. A beautiful sight to witness in downtown New York on any day and any season of the year.

Once I made it to the restaurant, I pulled up to have my car valet by a guy outside. The restaurant is on the top floor approximately on the top of the building with sky views and excellent ocean scenery over the whole city. I unlock my phone and proceed to send a text to iz "I'm on my way in." I type as I walk into the lobby entrance. It is a hotel/restaurant combined. The first floor seems to be quite busy as people are checking in and out, and attendants are assisting people with their stay. I approach the elevator and select the floor up button. "hello, I hope that you enjoy your time spent here, whether it is a hotel reservation or simply a nice dine in at our marvelous restaurant we appreciate you for choosing us!" the elevator says as it starts to incline up the floors. A few short minutes later, it stops and says "12th floor" the door then opens and reveals the restaurant. I stand in shock and preparation as I step out and into the floor to search for iz and proceed to our table.

As I motion my feet to enter into the floor and out of the elevator, I

The Unfaithful Woman

search for her in strength and confidence. as I look to my right, I have no sight of her. I look over to my left direction, and I see her on the inside sitting in the far back with her Away fuchsia dress, hair straightened and pulled behind her neck, with pumps on to match while on her cell phone. She had on nude lip gloss with a base nude eyeshadow. She looked damn well fantastic. Her legs and thighs were so vibrant and smooth that I wanted to lick them, so much that I wanted to lick and suck them both at the same time as a lollipop with cream filling, sucking it completely off the stick.

Staring at her, I felt this fire of no other than before. My dick became uncontrollably hard and rigid. All of my desires and emotions became wrapped into one. Tonight, would be an unpredictable mystery. I began to motion my feet to approach towards her. My eyes are locked on her sexiness and I am ready to become her king. "hello iz" I say to her as I reach our table area and get seated. "you weren't very hard to locate tonight." I say to her as I work my charm on her so that I could stun her, as she was that. she stared at me with her eyes budged, speechless for a second and then she responded as if she wanted to play it off.

"oh, thank you dave I wanted to look nice in here." She said laughing trying to hide her desire and her little break of her lip that almost turned into a grin once she had taken a good look at me. "So, let's have dinner shall we!" this would be a night to remember, and with that said we surely had to have a great meal on our stomach because tonight there was no telling what we might just get into, whether we were prepared or not. At least she wasn't, but I damn sure in the hell was.

Within five minutes of me getting seated the waitress approached us at our table. "Welcome, what may I get for you two tonight?" Iz and I locked eyes on each other, as if we were waiting on the other to go first. "you know, the ladies always are primary." I wonder what thoughts were going through her head. Was it the fact that I was so cool and smooth after everything? Or the fact that maybe she didn't want to reveal any emotion to me as she talked to me about what had happened, but either way there were some thoughts going through her head. One of many it seemed, not just one. "I will have the shrimp entrée buffet." "ok, what about you sir?" the waitress said after taking her order. "um, I think I will just have the porterhouse steak dinner with a side of salad as well."

"Anything to drink?" she rotated her head towards us to see which one of us would have an answer first. I looked at iz and nodded for her to make her choice first as I had said to her earlier. She decided to order a margarita and I chose to have champagne. "Ok, I will be back shortly with your meal!" as the waitress walked away from us to deliver our order iz and I began to lock eyes. "so, I have been waiting on you to talk to me." I gave her the vibe as if I knew how she had been feeling and it seemed to have made her even more shook, but she had to play it off hoping that I would not fully catch on to her little butterflies.

"yea, dave about that day; I have to be honest to tell you that I really do regret how I reacted. I should have thought it through and had a chance for you to state your offense before jumping off the gun at you, I sincerely apologize for that." "Fair enough baby I understand it was just in the heat of the moment." She stared at me as if she could not believe that I had forgiven her that easy. "Is it really that simple Dave?" "' Darling, it would be less of a man for me to hold something against you that would really be a fault of mine for not being honest with you, it made me feel like shit that I chose to keep it from you in the hopes that you wouldn't ever discover that part of me." "I can empathize with that Dave, I just wish you would have made that aware to me. I wonder if there is anything else that I should know about you. Discovering that had been so and you have not made that aware to me made me feel as if I had related with someone whom I thought that I knew this whole time but turned out to be a stranger to me." "I take full responsibility in that iz and I truly am sorry for not considering how that would make you feel from this point forward, It is my mission to be fully and whole truthful with you." It has made me feel very awful that I have not been completely and 100% honest with iz about my past and I do take full part as being selfish in the decision as choosing to withhold it from her.

"Thanks for that Dave I really appreciate that. you really are a nice man everything about you is just so contagious and irresistible." Did she just refer to me as "contagious" & "irresistible?" those are quite interesting words that she just described me as. "really, why don't you tell me what some of the things that make me contagious and irresistible?" "honestly dave, I have butterflies in my stomach when I imagine of revealing this to you. It's like with you, in a way I know that there is this connection

The Unfaithful Woman

that I have with you. This feeling that all is well. The kind of thing that I am protected, secure and I truthfully do not know how to react to that because it scares me."

"is that the alcohol talking, or is that how you have really felt?" I question her just to see what more she would say. I had her exactly where I wanted her, knowing that gives me the key to make her release her insecurities onto me. She needed to know that I wouldn't hurt her and I needed for her to give me the raw her, the her that she really is behind all of that boss phasad. "No, I really do feel secure it's like our energy takes control and I feel this instant connection with you that we are for each other. Like we are compatible and inseparable."

"iz you are so one of a kind to me. It's like god placed you on this planet and designed you just for me. Everything that you do is bold and its sexy. It's fierce less, with passion, and confidence. You are someone that I admire with an desire. Your strength is astonishing. Together, we can be an undeniable strength." I want her. I want to experience her. If I have to give my last to be with her, I will do anything to make sure that we get this chance. "so, what's after dinner?" she said to me as we finish our dessert. "you tell me, it's whatever you want to do I'm down for whatever." "I want you to lead the way, you're the man remember." "well, I guess I can show you how a man leads then huh?" "say we go back to my place, have a few more drinks, relax and watch the scenery." "that sounds like a great idea, no mind if I do."

XIII

Tonight is the night

We make it back to my place. I'm ready for her. I am going to do all the freaky shit that she needs, and she will like. The view is excellent, and the night is just beginning. "would you like some wine or champagne dear?" "I think I will take the wine." "let's go to the pool dear, but first let me get pool ready."

I head to my bedroom to grab some trunks and undress. "you can head now, I'm on my way behind you!" I shout as I start down the stairs to grab my glass of wine and head to the patio. "hey, I got my swimsuit on!" she says as she turns back around to see me. "Here I am baby" I come around the corner and stare as she sit on the edge of the pool with her baby blue one piece on. "You look absolutely stunning." "Come on, let's enjoy this moment." I walk towards her and start getting into the pool. "No problem, I'm already ready" I say to her with a desire to please and pursue.

"Get in" I reach for her. "One sec, I'm coming" she puts her hair up, takes my hand and descends into the pool. "So, I haven't asked you but how was your day?" "ugh, it was the usual bizarre day for me. Daily to-dos." "Are you exhausted?" I ask while I stare with concern and interest in what she has to say. "Heavily! I can't wait to just get my rest and relax tomorrow." "I want you to stay here with me, I hope you didn't think I would be wanting to let you leave did you?"

"you want me to stay? I guess so then, are you comfortable with that?" "why wouldn't I be??" "Idk…..i just…." She said with a look of uncertainty. "just what? What is it that's on your mind darling?" "maybe I just wasn't expecting this tonight, that's all." "let's continue to be unpredictable then shall we." "let's find out what's in store for us." "So, what are you feeling

The Unfaithful Woman

now?" "I'm wondering what's your plan right now, that's what I'm thinking about." She says with a burst of laughter. "what do you mean what my plan is, is there something in particular that's on your mind?" "The water really feels great, I can feel the soothing sensation through my body." She changed the subject from answering my question, but I think I know exactly what she is thinking about, and I am going to give her just that.

I'll go with the flow for now. "yea, it definitely does, I needed a night like this after a busy day I've had." "HA! I had an enormous amount of work to do, so much that it was unbelievable." "That is most relatable." "did you get back to work today? I didn't cause you to lose your job did i? that wasn't my intention, I was just really disappointed and caught up into my emotions." "it's not a problem baby, stop feeling guilty about that. nothing happened." "were you embarrassed? I feel like I really did embarrassed you." "Stop with the guilt, everything is fine."

"Ok, I'll just stop now I just feel like I fucked up majorly and I want to apologize." "how many times do you feel the need to apologize to me iz? It's ok, let it go, let's move on." "I'm ready to take a shower now, relax, maybe watch a good film what about you?" "sure, you can go ahead I'll wait until you finish and then I will go." "I'm sorry, but did you not just hear what I just implied?" "what, you said you wanted to shower right?" "there's one thing that you're missing, I want you in it with me, and not just myself." She sits and stares at me with hesitation to speak, I reach and grab for her hand. "come on, let's go."

I reach for our towels to dry us off before we enter from outside of the patio into the condo. First, I dry her off and rap the towel around her, then myself and we head inside. Up the stairs we went, into the master bedroom. "Take off your clothes, I'll get the water ready." I say. I head towards the shower and turn on the water and music. I drop all my clothes slowly to the floor, pacing around the corner to signal for her to come to me. "it's ready for us now." I use my fingers to wave her towards me. "you look stunning, we need to wash up and get fresh."

Into the shower, first I go then her in front of me. "do you trust me?" I ask her while rubbing her body down and whispering in her ear. Kissing on her neck and sucking with my lips. "tell me how much you want me." I start my fingers towards her clit, "say my name" I whisper. "don't you ever forget me, I'm your ultimate daddy." At this point I have her moaning and wanting. "yes!" she says aloud moaning and screeching. Grabbing the shower door and walls in pleasure and excitement as I please her. "tell me that you trust me, I want to know that I have your full attention and security. Give me your permission to fuck you like never before." "Uh! Yes! Give me all of it now!" I lower down to her thighs and start slurping & eating her pussy out. "YES! More! She screams" the more she wanted, the more I gave to her. Harder and rougher I went until she tapped out and squirted everywhere.

I ate most of it and then I came up, turned her around and looked her in the eye. "now, it's time for you to show me appreciation. Daddy wants you to show him that he is important to you. Go!" I MOTION HER HEAD Downwards to my dick. She looks up at me from my dick, I smile at her and nod for her to go to work on me. When she starts, I instantly feel a unpredictable and indescribable tingle at my penis.

She's lightly biting and sucking my dick. At this point my dick is bulging like a volcano. She twittles her tongue on the head, I instantly start to feel a muscle contraction coming on. I stoop down and grab her by her waist and ass, lift her up, and then start to enter her. As I slide into her walls, she says "Slow down, not so quick!" I slide my hands further down her back and let her fall backwards to the shower floor and then I begin to stroke her out. "Dave!" Grabbing the walls and scratching the glass. "you're so hard! Fuck me!" "you want papi's cum?" teasing her in the ear, licking and kissing on her. "yes"

Almost there, about to make the touchdown I swiftly pull out and pull her head back down to me dick. "you want it here" I say to her with my dick pointed at her mouth, stroking to masturbate. "yes." In not even three seconds, I start to feel my muscles contract. I explode all over and into her mouth. She takes the end of me and finish the rest of what's left on my head. "so, you like that kind of thing?" I ask. "what do you mean?" she asks while staring up at me with a look of pleasure and satisfaction. "swallowing, you like to do that kind of thing?" "I have a confession to make to you now, this is the first time that I've done that ever." "Are you serious? You've never done what I just did to you before??" "No, no one has ever shown me what you just did, it's all new to me."

I grab her around her waist and bring her close to me. "you ready to go to the bedroom?" "" Sure" "put your legs around me" I picked her up, slid the door, and took her to the bedroom. There was a feeling of shifting. She held onto me like she trusted me with her dear life. She seemed to have been tired out, so I laid her down, put a kiss on her cheek. "you seem exhausted darlin, goodnight and sleep tight." "I want you to hold me. I want to feel you close to me." She said softly while tapping into rest mode. I get into bed, wrap my arms around her, and begin to embrace her. "I want to thank you for tonight, I appreciate it." "you appreciate everything, huh?" "hypothetically speaking, honestly yes." With a burst of laughter. "Did I hurt you??"

"Are you asking the question so boldly right now?" screaming with laughter while rising out of her position to look direct towards me. "what, i'm just making sure my baby is ok. I know it got pretty crazy." "honestly, the way you handled me is really impressive. I like a man who can take control of me." "will you trust me now?" "dave, I can trust you I just need for you to be completely and mutually honest with me as I will with you."

Bingo, I have her right where I want her. "I agree to that and also to have the communication." I made A Big mistake, I understand that and now moving forward I know that I have to be honest. She is important to me and I don't want to hurt her.

XIV

Tying the knot

On April 5 came our incredibly special day. Everyone gathering on this day, at this moment for this special occasion. The scene covered in roses and turquoise with blue trimming accents. All the women with their turquoise gown and the men in their ocean blue suits. All my co-workers were here, in support of me. The weather was warm and breezy.

We all stood, here and waiting on the special person, the bride to be, my iz. We waited 8 months eagerly for this memorable day. I proposed to her on the island in the Caribbean, where we had taken vacation for a few weeks. Months it had taken for us to plan and follow through with this getaway because work had us tied down. The scenery and the ocean were astounding, we never wanted to leave. It was like heaven on earth. There was no such thing as being busy or occupied, it was all leisure almost a place for retirement people to live either permanently or indefinitely.

It had taken us over 18 hours to get there and after a certain point, we had to take a helicopter for the remainder of the way. I'd planned a whole scene on the last night of our getaway to propose. On the beach I had set up a table for us with roses, music, candles with wine and champagne. We ate dinner, which was excellent the chef were on point with the dessert and everything overall definitely met my expectations.

At the end of having our last dinner there, I had the group of men to come out to sing. The group were by the name of color me badd, from which they gave and intimacy vibe to the night. She became emotional and anxious once she saw me kneel onto one knee at her and propose. Just like that, she bursts into tears, accepted my proposal, and all was sealed.

Now, today we are here and we are about to seal the deal once and for all together for eternity. Her eyes and skin are glowing with excitement and overwhelm. we are all in our positions and the horns begin to blow and the music beings to play.

"it seems like forever, that I have waited for you."

Johnny gill sings as the curtains get ready to unravel and reveal my woman to me as she walks down the aisle.

She's absolutely stunning in her turquoise gown, her hair pinned in a curvy bon with her nude lip gloss. We stare at each other as she gets closer to me. I have waited for this day and now that it is here, It feels all like a fairytale. We smile at each other with tears doom to fall below our eyelids.

I didn't notice that my grandmother were here with my mother until I glanced over at her. I do not know how she were able to speak with my mother for her to know about my day but she was here. I couldn't believe it, I had not saw her in at least a good 9 years. My brother & father were still missing as I would have liked to have my whole family here but my mother being present made it even more sentimental to me. As you know, my brother is in rehab finally as I had hoped for him to seek help for a long time so at least he is somewhere curing himself.

"All of you may be seated." The pastor says. "I know the two of you wanted to just say what was on your heart. So I will just let you guys start."

Our eyes lock and iz has tears rolling down her face as she observes me in awe, so I decide to let her go first.

"I never thought that I could meet someone like you....when I look at you, I think how in a million years could this man have found interest in little old me?? It was like god stationed the two of us where we were until we met with each other because he designed you just for me. You pulled me out of the darkness and brought me into the light." "I can say this no matter what we go through or what we endure in this life, I do know that I will always love you. You are my smile, my knight and shining armor, you are my everything."

With tears in her eyes those were her words and neither of us could believe that we were it. Just two people from two separate lives with two separate backgrounds but we had an inseparable connection. It was unexplainable, we were intertwined with each other.

"Isabella Claire." Staring at her with love all over me and I could feel the guests must have felt this as well. "when I first laid eyes onto you my darlin, I said to myself she's different and unlike any woman I have come encounter with before. I knew somehow you would change my life but I guess I was a little naive as to how tremendously you would become meaningfully in my life. I love you is and I want you forever and with me until the end. My little sunflower, my little sweet peach."

"after this, there is nothing more to say you may kiss your bride." The minister says to me as we lock lips and seal to deal to being as one and whole forever. Mr. and Mrs. shubbard.

XV

Life after

Five years into tying the knot on our love and our marriage seems to be on a strange level. We have become strained without an legitimate reason. We barely make love anymore, maybe it's us working a lot. Or, maybe the same routine has gotten worn, but it's really quite strange. The connection that we once shared, seems to have faded away. It hurts because it feels that I have failed but will we ever be the same is the question. A part of me feels that she is having an affair on me but I don't want to jump to conclusions. She's out late on a regular and says that she has work late. Is that just an excuse for me to believe, or could she really be telling the truth. She doesn't call me from the office and talk with me the entire hour like before during her lunch break. When she's home she often spends more time on the patio drinking wine; on her phone than with me where we used to talk and nurture the both of us.

    I often lie beside her in bed and reside over the things that could've put us onto the path of disconnection. However, tonight took a devastating turn. She was sound asleep beside me when I hear her phone going off miraculously. Beep beep beep beep beep beep beep it kept going and going. She was in such a deep sleep that she didn't hear or notice it. Curious to know who this phone call was from I began to reach for her phone. The screen read incoming call from an unknown number that I wasn't aware of. "Hello" I answered as I was curious as to who would be calling as unknown, especially at this time of night. To my curiosity, no one would answer. I could feel m heart drop and my stomach sunk. I know whoever it was heard my voice and knew it wasn't her and disconnected the call. I was awake the whole night disturbed by that phone call.

I had finally fell off to sleep sometime in the morning leading up to sunrise. When I had woken up she was gone and the apartment was silent. I could hear a pin drop to the floor. I live 50 floors above ground, so I barely hear traffic and noise unless I went out onto the balcony. I wanted to lie in the bed for the remainder of my day and just drown into my emotions, but I couldn't because for one I had work and two I wanted answers. My mind is going a million miles a minute. What did I do to deserve to be stepped out on, why wouldn't she just be honest about what she was missing from our marriage that triggered her to do this? I have received complete betrayal from her and I am quite furious. It makes me believe that everything we shared was complete bogus.

Whoever this mystery man is must be keeping her quite happy. All the attention has left me and onto this man. I need more information did she meet this guy at work, online, or what and where did this side guy become apart of her life. I look over at my alarm clock and it reads 1 pm. It's one of those dark and gloomy days, matches the vibe that is casted over my life right now.

I proceed to exit my bed and start my what is normally identified AS A normal day but really is a shit show scene of my life. The same routine as is every day I go to my closet, decide what to wear, lay it all out, and proceed to my shower. Today, the only difference was that I decided to wear polo shirt and slacks when I normally choose a suit. Just in case I may have to beat a mutha-fucker on the ass. The adrenaline in me was at it's peak. The pain was turning into heated anger. This was something that I needed to meditate away and think through clearly.

I was so distraught & pissed at the same time. I didn't even want to leave my place. The day was as usual with the high and busy morning traffic. The roads were filled with people walking across street to street and building to building in their umbrellas and drench coats. However, today was slightly different than usual. There was this man as I was leaving my condo heading to my parking garage who was sitting on the bench. He didn't seem like he was waiting for anything, he looked homeless. He was dressed in joggers that looked as if they had not been washed in months and an blue sweater which had multiple dark spots. He had long hair that looked had been a while since he'd had not had a touchup in quite some time with a long black beard. He had an empty open can and as people walked by most would drop some change in for him. I empathized for him. I reached for my wallet and in cash I had about $300. So, I just walked up to him. "Hello," with concern and curiosity of why he was here and what his story is.

"what brings you here today, are you ok? You look like you have been through something rough." He just looked at me with a blank expression. He formed what could've become a laugh, but was just a small giggle. "Life has brought me here." He said with a quick pause. " Thing and circumstances in my life that was unexpected and unfair happened to me, so it has brought me here. I feel so helpless and worthless being this low. I feel embarrassed of how I am viewed by people. I never imagined that it would come to this in my life."

"do you mind if I ask what you story is?" as I sit beside him with concern and care to hear what his journey was that lead him to hear, he starts to form tears in his eyes. A pause and sigh he begins to talk to me.

"when the economy crashed, I lost everything. All of my money was gone, I lost my home and assets due to foreclosure and delinquency. It was just like a big hurricane. What I worked for one by one was taken from me. I just only could sit and watch it all fall apart. There was nothing I could do. I had no one to truly help me. It hurt."

I stared at him and just was in awe. I received an epiphany. "may I ask your name man?" I asked him just for the record.

"connor, my name is connor."

In that moment I knew that there had been so much more to embrace in life that my little problem right now. I could be in this situation or worse. It only takes half of a second for your life to drastically transform.

"so, connor you seem like a nice man." I reached into my wallet and gave him all the cash I had.

"I would like to get you cleaned up, maybe get you some nice food. Where is it that you live? I know a shelter nearby that can take you in and help you get on your feet. They have this program where you can get back on track with your occupation and everything to where you can be stable again."

He turned and looked at me with a slight look of disinterest.

"you know, I wonder if I were to get back to the way things were if it would happen to me again. That's a concern that I have, I lost so much is it all worth loosing again?"

Hearing him say this made me have a mutual connection with him. Considering I have lost my wife has truly made me feel worthless and less of a man. You can have it all and then you can have it slip through your fingers. The only thing is, I tried to be the good and attentive husband that was and is needed in a marriage. I helped this woman through poverty and gave her effortless access to a world that most people only dream of. Only the universe knows where this will go from here.

"man, I understand your position fully and I empathize with you but you have to know that there are ups and downs and stumbles that we will acquire in life and you just have to get back up and try again. If this is the hardest you've fallen this far, just think about how great your comeback will be."

"Where is it that I would even begin to start? I mean, I'm sure that I could get back to my career, but a place, clothes, shoes, just how?"

I looked into his eyes with assurance.

"trust me, I can help you."

Getting up from the bench while I extend my hand out to help him up.

"First, we should get to a near washeteria and get you all cleaned and tidy up and then while that's being done we can head to the nearest mall and I'll help you get some clothes and we can get ya washed up."

I took him to most popular and exquisite salon in the area, "synclaire's!" it's owned by a nice woman named Claire. She comes from a history of wealth through her family and basically just gets to sit on her ass and do everything that she wants to do. Her family were successful farmers and landowners. She can be a very useful asset when it comes to connections and getting things done.

"Hi dave!"

Her eyes sparkled with excitement and enthusiasm once she looked up and witnessed that it was me walking through the door.

"what can I do for ya today bud!"

She was always excited to see me, we have great conversation and laughs together and we just get each other. I've been going to her salon for years now.

"I have someone here today Claire, I am helping them out and I need to get them fixed up and freshened up."

She looks at him and nods her head towards me with a wink.

"Don't mind if I do dave!"

"once your done with everything just give me a call and charge it to me. I will be back shortly."

"okie doke!"

"she's going to get you touched up and cleaned up so when you walk out of here you will look like a million bucks! I will go and find you a nice wardrobe and will be back as a swift as I can."

At this point all that I wanted to do was uplift him and make him feel encouraged, happy, and that he was cared for. I wanted him to feel and know that he had a team of people on his side that would stand with him through the way as he regains his lifestyle & courage back. There's a boutique a few blocks by the name of "dedra's." she has the best selection of quality clothing and a little something for every occasion. So, I will just pick up a little for every scenario. It is owned by a lady who does wholesale and makes a little bit of her own clothing line. Dedra has several locations over the state that are well established and sponsored by notable platforms. This location happens to be one of the largest and grand spots that she has. I walk in and I immediately have to decide which section to choose first. So many brands to select with a number of options to devour in.

"hi! Welcome to dedra's! anything in particular that you are in search for today??"

"I'm on a mission to transform someone. I want to enhance them into a new man. A look that says yea I'm all of that, but I'm also transparent to you."

"we have just the thing here. A little preppy but gives a little hello to it. Basically, I'm the guy that can provide, but I'm definitely approachable don't be afraid."

"yea, I like the sound of that. you're speaking my exact language."

She guided me over to the cute & elegant section. Good smelling cologne, top branded and well glossed shoes, jeans and tops stitched from the high-quality Egyptian cotton. Of course, every piece of clothing and fabric in the store were worth three c notes and up. By c notes, I mean hundreds of dollars. The good thing is that it lasts a long time. On the other hand, if you're highly privileged and successful like me you'll probably only wear it once. In this case, he needed something that will lasts him for now that he could possibly wear over just for the time being. He has more to be worried about that clothing. That can all come later.

"I am looking for something that he can have a longer span with as far as quality at the same time. He needs to be able to wear this multiple times at least while he is getting himself back on the correct track financially. He's had a bit of financial hardship after the recession, and he lost a lot."

She turns to me in concern

"that's very sad to hear. I know quite a few people that went through a tough time due to that crash.. we are always willing to help here as much as we can. It takes a village and we empathize with everyone who has been affected in any way."

"it's good to know. It's crazy how one minute your life can be at one level and then it can flash and dissolve right before your eyes without a say so or even a finger can be lifted to stop or control it."

"oh yes, you just have to keep trying and keep pushing on this journey called life. Believe me, I know a thing or two. It's all a part of the process, you just must trust it all. And live by the moment."

XVI

The wreak of havoc

I spent over two hours making sure that he had everything that he needed. I feel like I have done a great deed today. One that taught me a great lesson. Just to think while I was out lending a hand to a person in need, my own wife was betraying me. She is betraying me every single second that this affair is going on. At this point I'm so numb that I really can't even wrap my head around this whole thing. I should've been at work hours ago, but after all I was doing something productive. Instead of going to the dinery that I always go to before work which is one the opposite side of town close to the tower, I decided to just stop at this one near to where I am now because It would be quicker and I could just go straight into work.

I like to have a nice Frappuccino and a bagel every morning, nothing has changed so I'll do the same this day. I park my car on the curb and walk to enter the diner. Just walking in and smelling the freshly brewed coffee and the warm dough uplifts my spirit. It took five minutes to receive my order which still turned out to be swifter than across town at this time. As I turned to grab a straw and lid for my frapp, I glanced out the window. The more I focused, the more it seemed like I recognized these two people. They were walking and holding hands on the crosswalk from one side of the street to the other. Laughing and smiling they were it looked like my wife. As the wind blew hair, she twisted her head and just enough to the right to where I could recognize that it was her.

The man that she was with looked quite noticeable let alone. By this time, they were too far on the opposite direction for me to define who she was with. The only way to find out for sure is to follow them. I quickly rushed out of the diner and charged towards my car trail after them. It's obvious that my car could be spotted, so I will have to just linger in the distance. Now thinking that it may have been best to walk, but I'm not sure how far I would be walking or if I would end up losing track of them In the crowd. Knowing who this other man could be is going to give me the closure, one that will help me to just move on because I'm sure there's probably something in him that I haven't acquired to make her commit this betrayal in our marriage. I want to be able to look him eye to eye, man to man and get the truth. They're in my vision path fairly as I turned onto the corner. Holding hands as they still were as if they were riding off onto the sunset. They must've walked halfway down the strip before making a turn and into the region they went. The region is an prominent and exquisite hotel that is mainly occupied with business and wealthy clients. She wasn't looking to notice that I wasn't far behind them. They entered the twisting door of what is considered the entrance door of the hotel. As they proceeded to the desk, I slowly entered behind them listening for the information that I needed to acquire this truth.

"here is your reservation, room 43, you guys enjoy your stay!"

The secretary said to them and they headed towards the elevator. Of course, I had to figure the floor that held room 43 beside the elevator had a poster of directory of where every area of the hotel would be. Room 43 is held on the fourth floor. Just as I started toward the elevator there was a woman who had tapped the floor up button to the elevator which was just the option I wanted to choose. As the door opened, we both entered inside she chose floor seven and I chose floor four which would make my stop first. It made two stops before landing to floor four, one at floor two and floor three.

Once I got to floor four and the elevator doors opened it revealed a quiet hallway. One so quiet you could hear the crickets chirping or a pin drop as some would say. I walked out of the doors and turned to my right. After a few seconds of noticing that the numbers were only increasing 46, 47, 48, I made a u turn and went in the opposite direction. It was still very much silent on this floor not a person moving in and out or so much of a bump of a door. Room 43 was only arm's length away. I deeply in my soul, felt that I would be hearing moaning and sexual noises but there was only dead silence. As I approached the door to room 43 I hear a door snap close and I hear feet clamp down the hall. They were headed in my direction as the footsteps became louder and more definable. I turned and skimped around the corner from the elevator, up against the wall waiting to peep around if the ghost became clear.

It had to of been them because a door shut once again not too far from the room. I dashed around the wall to glance in the hall. There was not a person or an object in sight. This meant the ghost was clear. Now, it's time to figure out what is really going on here. Which it seems perfectly clear, no excuses. I went to open the door carefully and diligently, but the door is locked as I assumed it would be. There is only one or two ways to have it opened. Number one would be to use the known and infamous hair pin trick and pry it open, while number two would be to get the staff to open it up. Conflicted on the most stable move I should make I drastically chose to go with number one and use a hair pin to silently open up the door.

I used my elbow to reach down into my coat pocket where I kept them for keeps when I had my mullet and flow look going on. After shuffling around what would be maybe about 5 hair pins in my pocket I caught onto one itself and retracted it from my pocket. I angled and shaped it to fixate onto the doorknob carefully while turning the handle. Luckily this wasn't the type of door to create noise or friction while opening it, not that it mattered at this point anyway because everything would be exposed by now but the idea of having the chance of visually seeing it without no one getting a chance to disregard the act they were into in that moment was what I wanted. I want it just how it is in the moment it's in.

The door had swung open to a clear view and walkway. There wasn't any noises that I expected to hear, but there was some conversation being had between the two. Curious to ease drop on what the details were, I let the door close shut to a minimum click of the lock and stood against the wall to listen. Isabella started to utter with disdain from her mouth.

"I've felt so guilty about this since the first day this has started. You and I both know that we are caught up in something that could get really, really ugly."

"of course, we both know how catastrophic this could get. There is a lot at stake here iz, I am fully aware of that."

"one day we are going to get caught and this will not be good. it is bound to happen, we need to make a decision to do whatever to end this love triangle."

He called her iz like I did. I wonder if he felt the same about her as I did. Of course, now my feelings have altered and how I view her is filled with nothing more than bitter and resentment. Did he see her as beautiful and unique to himself as I did, or was she just a piece of pussy to him that he picked up? Those were the thoughts running through my mind as I continued to ease in on this conversation but It seemed much, much deeper than just an ordinary affair. It seemed to be tangling, or an entanglement one might call it.

"if he ever finds out about you, I'm not sure if we even would or should be known to him. It would be the smart thing to leave. Us ever having anything more than this is completely dead so that's a gone with the wind consideration."

"do you really care that much what happened of what will happen? What's wrong with living in our own truth no matter what the repercussions will be it would just have to be accepted."

The voice seemed very familiar. The more I listened the more the voice became more knowingly and knowingly defining but I just couldn't quite put my finger on the exact answer. They weren't whispering but they also weren't screaming either so I couldn't really exactly make a judgment.

"for god sakes! Have some moral and remorse! You are his brother! How do you think that would make him feel?! Do you think I am really some evil person like that?!"

"what did you just say???!"

I jumped from around the corner and saw a full image of exactly who and what I wanted to see, but all that I saw wasn't who I expected to see for sure. I didn't expect to see my brother. My blood brother that we share not only parents, memories, and a life with, but pure red blood and genes. This whole time it had been him who was sleeping with my wife. All my emotions came down at once, I wasn't sure which emotion I should or wanted to feel and I couldn't control which of them entered the room to start.

"so, what was the motive?"

This is all that I could say at this point given that I was in such of a shock; not only about him, but both he and my wife whom I adored and never would fathom would bring this kind of pain and betrayal to me.

"go ahead, I'm waiting you picked this way to hurt me because you resent me don't you? You really want to see me at my worst don't you?"

The Unfaithful Woman

He stared at me as if he didn't want to say a word because he had gotten caught up, they both had gotten caught up in their nasty deed. He was frozen. I didn't take my eyes from off of him and I wonder if he could visually see the pain that dwelled inside of me. After taking a long look at me he turned his eyes to iz for a split second and then turned back to me.

"no David, that is not what I wanted to do here. We have been through our ups and downs, but this is something that I never intentionally would ever have wanted to cause to happen to you. Sitting here looking at you I know there is nothing that I can say that could change this and I only can just say that I have tremendously caused a big fuck up. I have caused a big fuck up in your marriage and played a part that has been very ugly."

"how long has this been going on? When did you even get out of the facility?"

"David I have been out for about 8 months now and I am doing better. I started seeing someone to help me through my wounds that I was referred to after exiting rehab but David I have regretfully fallen for your wife and I feel like complete shit. I had hopes of repairing things with us, but I have only caused more damage one that may be of no repair with this. I know you don't want to even hear my sorry."

I didn't really know what to say in this moment or how to respond, but I was deeply hurt. I felt like a fool. One for love as the old cliché states.

"your wish is my command."

I looked at both of them in complete calmness and disappointment.

"isabella, bon voyage it was nice while it was. Your belongings will be brought to you by my assistant, there's no need to see each other any further than here today."

I turned and left the room. I am so done and over this betrayal that I am willing to give whatever it takes to not be ashamed like this again. If there's one thing for sure in life is that you win and you lose. Not everything that comes into your life is meant to be forever lasting. For with ever loss, there is a gain and more to gain in the future. Live and let life live you.

THE END

Made in the USA
Monee, IL
22 June 2022

98437190R00037